For my family, with love

Published in Canada by Tundra Books, a division of Random House of Canada Limited,
One Toronto Street, Suite 300, Toronto, Ontario M5C 2V6

Published in the United States by Tundra Books of Northern New York,
P.O. Box 1030, Plattsburgh, New York 12901

Library of Congress Control Number: 2013953671

Library and Archives Canada Cataloguing in Publication

Côté, Geneviève, 1964–, author, illustrator
    Bob's hungry ghost / written and illustrated by Geneviève Côté.

Issued in print and electronic formats.
ISBN 978-1-77049-713-9 (bound).—ISBN 978-1-77049-714-6 (epub)

    I. Title.

PS8605.O8738B62 2014   jC813'.6   C2013-906900-3
                                                C2013-906901-1

Edited by Tara Walker
Designed by Leah Springate
The artwork in this book was rendered in mixed media.
The text was set in Balance.

www.tundrabooks.com

Printed and bound in China

1 2 3 4 5 6   19 18 17 16 15 14

BOB'S HUNGRY GHOST

GENEVIÈVE CÔTÉ

TUNDRA BOOKS

Bob has a ghost.
He really wanted a dog.
Or a cat. Or even a gerbil.
But Bob got a ghost for his birthday, and he called it Fluffy.

The ghost thinks Fluffy is a silly name. But it doesn't matter what Bob calls him since Fluffy never listens anyway. When Bob says, "Fetch, Fluffy, fetch!" or "Sit, Fluffy, sit!" Fluffy doesn't move an inch.

Ghosts don't like to fetch at all. And they can't actually sit.

Walking a ghost on a leash isn't a very good idea either. Fluffy can't walk. BUT he sure can fly!

He is also good at hide-and-seek.

Too bad Bob doesn't seem to like it.

Fluffy wonders what to do. He glows in the dark for a while . . . but it isn't much fun when no one is watching. Fluffy is getting bored.

He starts munching on a book.
Ghosts are awfully hungry when
they're bored.

And hungry ghosts will eat ANYTHING!

Fluffy is getting BIGGER and BIGGER.

Things keep disappearing around the house.
Bob is puzzled. "Have you seen my teapot?" he asks.
"Have you seen my clock? And is it my imagination, or
have you gotten rather BIG?"

Fluffy shrugs and tries to look as innocent as a lamb.
Ghosts hardly look like lambs.

Soon the house is almost empty.
Bob doesn't notice Fluffy
looming CLOSER and
CLOSER...

Bob spins and swirls and lands
with a loud THUMP.

"What happened?" He looks
around. "*There's* my teapot! And
my clock and ALL my things!"

But everything seems different,
glowing palely in the dark.

"Why, they're as pale as . . .

. . . a GHOST!"

Bob is *inside* Fluffy's belly!
"Bad ghost!" he calls out.
"Bad, BAD ghost!"

There is no answer from Fluffy
except a loud

"BURP!"

"Oh well." Bob sighs. He finds some hot chocolate,
settles in his armchair and picks up a book,
The Big Book of Ghosts. He begins to read:

*Although they cannot walk or sit, ghosts love
to fly. They can appear and disappear, glow
in the dark and go through walls. Ghosts are
VERY special.*
*But if your ghost doesn't feel welcome in
your house, watch out for mischief!*

"Hmm . . . " Bob thinks. "Ghosts sure are special."

"Hmm . . . " Fluffy thinks too.

Now he has nothing left to eat and no friend to play with.

Fluffy misses Bob. He even misses all that sitting and fetching nonsense. Besides, eating Bob wasn't a very nice thing to do.

Fluffy takes a deep breath and
opens his mouth as wide as a door.
Bob jumps out.

Bob looks at Fluffy.
Fluffy looks at Bob.
Bob cracks a smile . . .

. . . and Fluffy giggles.
He laughs so hard that
he spits out ALL of
Bob's things.

Now Fluffy is never bored
and feels at home with Bob.
Together they play ball . . .

and hide-and-seek . . .

. . . and read bedtime stories.

Especially ghost stories.

Bob thinks EVERYONE should get a ghost for their birthday!